INSIDE MAJOR LEAGUE BASEBALL™

BASEBALL IN THE NATIONAL LEAGUE EAST DIVISION

ATLANTA
BRAVES

FLORIDA
MARLINS

NEW YORK
METS

PHILADELPHIA
PHILLIES

WASHINGTON
NATIONALS

rosen publishing's
rosen central®

New York

JASON PORTERFIELD

Published in 2009 by The Rosen Publishing Group, Inc.
29 East 21st Street, New York, NY 10010

Library of Congress Cataloging-in-Publication Data

Porterfield, Jason.
Baseball in the National League East Division / Jason Porterfield.—1st ed.
    p. cm.—(Inside Major League Baseball)
Includes bibliographical references and index.
ISBN-13: 978-1-4358-5043-9 (library binding)
ISBN-13: 978-1-4358-5417-8 (pbk)
ISBN-13: 978-1-4358-5423-9 (6 pack)
1. National League of Professional Baseball Clubs—Juvenile literature. 2. Baseball teams—United States—Juvenile literature. I. Title.
GV875.A3P67 2009
796.357'640973—dc22

                                                                    2008022284

Manufactured in the United States of America

On the cover: Baseball cards, top to bottom: Chipper Jones of the Atlanta Braves; Hanley Ramirez of the Florida Marlins; David Wright of the New York Mets; Ryan Howard of the Philadelphia Phillies; and Ryan Zimmerman of the Washington Nationals. Background: Citizens Bank Park in Philadelphia, Pennsylvania. Center: Johan Santana of the New York Mets.

CONTENTS

INTRODUCTION 4

CHAPTER ONE
Baseball in the NL East 7

CHAPTER TWO
Managing in the NL East 13

CHAPTER THREE
NL East Winners and Rivals 18

CHAPTER FOUR
NL East Players 26

CHAPTER FIVE
Baseball Tradition in the NL East 35

GLOSSARY 41

FOR MORE INFORMATION 42

FOR FURTHER READING 44

BIBLIOGRAPHY 45

INDEX 47

NOV 7 – 2009

INTRODUCTION

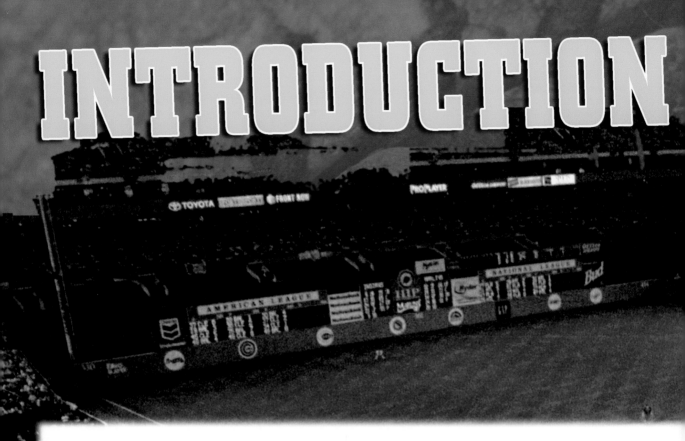

I n the 2003 World Series, the Florida Marlins of the National League East division faced a strong New York Yankees team. The American League champions had finished the season with the best record in baseball; the underdog Marlins hadn't even won their division. However, the Marlins led the series three games to two going into game 6, with staff ace Josh Beckett scheduled to start. Beckett, on just three days' rest, pitched a complete game shutout to win 2–0 and lead Florida to its second World Series championship in six years.

A lot of baseball fans were surprised by the Marlins' success. For fans that follow the teams of the National League East, however, the outcome of the 2003 World Series was almost routine. The division's teams—the Atlanta Braves, Florida Marlins, New York Mets, Philadelphia Phillies, and Washington Nationals—have played in six World Series since 1994, winning three. The Braves made three of those appearances during their incredible 11-year run as division champions. The Mets and Marlins have also gone to the World Series,

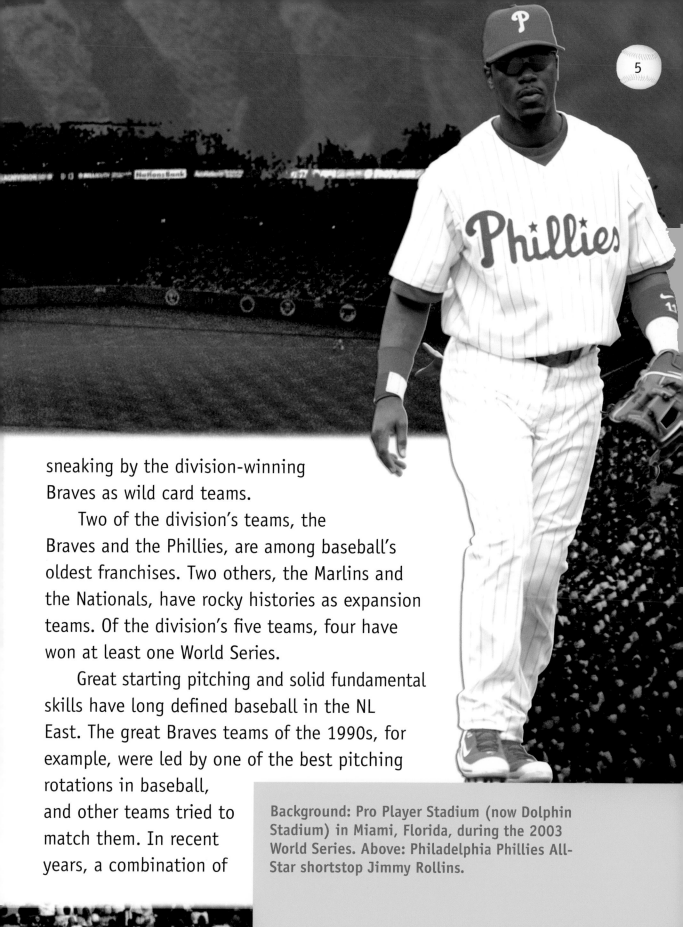

5

sneaking by the division-winning Braves as wild card teams.

Two of the division's teams, the Braves and the Phillies, are among baseball's oldest franchises. Two others, the Marlins and the Nationals, have rocky histories as expansion teams. Of the division's five teams, four have won at least one World Series.

Great starting pitching and solid fundamental skills have long defined baseball in the NL East. The great Braves teams of the 1990s, for example, were led by one of the best pitching rotations in baseball, and other teams tried to match them. In recent years, a combination of

Background: Pro Player Stadium (now Dolphin Stadium) in Miami, Florida, during the 2003 World Series. Above: Philadelphia Phillies All-Star shortstop Jimmy Rollins.

speed and power has become more important in the division, as the Mets and Phillies have achieved success as offense-oriented teams. Read on to learn more about the teams and players who make baseball in the National League East division so much fun to watch.

CHAPTER ONE
BASEBALL IN THE NL EAST

The National League, formed in 1876, was one of the first professional baseball leagues established in the United States. After the 1899 season, the league eliminated three less-successful teams, leaving a core of eight teams. These franchises would become popular as the Boston Braves, Brooklyn Dodgers, Chicago Cubs, Philadelphia Phillies, Cincinnati Reds, New York Giants, Pittsburgh Pirates, and St. Louis Cardinals.

Hall of Fame third baseman Mike Schmidt *(left)* became a Phillies legend playing in the 1970s and 1980s. Find out more about Schmidt on page 27.

Boston Pilgrims fans swarm the field after their team beat the Pittsburgh Pirates in the first World Series, in 1903. The Pilgrims became today's Red Sox.

Teams in the rival American League started competing in 1901. And, in 1903, the two leagues played against each other in the first major league World Series.

Baseball changed dramatically in the next few decades. For example, the pitcher-dominated Dead Ball Era ended in the 1920s, with the arrival of such sluggers as Babe Ruth and Hack Wilson. Later, in the 1940s, Jackie Robinson of the Brooklyn Dodgers finally opened up the major leagues to African American players. Despite these changes, the team lineup of the National League changed very little. Then, in 1953, the Boston Braves moved to Milwaukee, becoming the Milwaukee Braves. More shifts followed, as the Brooklyn Dodgers and New York Giants relocated to California in 1958. The Milwaukee Braves would move again in 1966, this time to Atlanta.

Expansion and Division Play

The National League also added several teams. In 1962, the Houston Colt .45s (who later became the Houston Astros) and the New York Mets joined. Then, in 1969, the league added the San Diego Padres and the Montreal Expos. The Expos became the first major league team based in Canada.

Also in 1969, both the American League and the National League split into East and West divisions. This allowed more teams to compete for a chance at the play-offs. The six teams in the original NL East included the Montreal Expos, New York Mets, Philadelphia Phillies, Pittsburgh Pirates, Chicago Cubs, and St. Louis Cardinals. The team with the best record in the division at the end of the season was the division champion. This team then played the winner of the NL West division in a best-of-five National League Championship Series (NLCS). The winner of the NLCS advanced to play against the American League champion in the World Series.

The 1994 Realignment

In 1994, Major League Baseball formed two new divisions: the AL Central and the NL Central. These divisions provided a chance to straighten out some of the quirks of the old divisions. For example, the Atlanta

The "Miracle Mets" of 1969

During the early 1960s, the New York Mets were known for their inept play, losing 120 games in their first season. Late in the 1969 season, things seemed to be going no differently for the team. They were stuck in third place in mid-August, ten games behind the division-leading Chicago Cubs. The Mets then began one of baseball's greatest comebacks, winning 38 of their last 49 games to clinch the NL East championship in their first winning season.

The Mets were considered underdogs in the National League Championship Series, where they faced a powerful Atlanta Braves team led by home run king Hank Aaron. Surprisingly, the Mets swept the Braves in three games to advance to the World Series. There, they faced a mighty Baltimore Orioles team that had gone 109–53 in the regular season. New York's ace, Tom Seaver, lost the first game, but the "Miracle Mets" didn't give up hope. They regrouped to beat the Orioles in game 2. They also won game 3, with young flame-thrower Nolan Ryan pitching three innings of shutout ball to earn the save. Seaver came back to lead the Mets to a game 4 victory. With their game 5 win, the Mets completed their amazing season, taking home their first World Series championship.

Tom Seaver began his Hall of Fame career with the New York Mets. He earned the nickname "Tom Terrific" for his excellence on the mound.

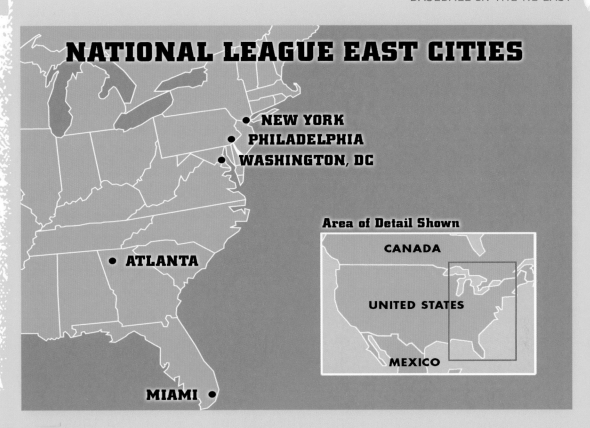

NATIONAL LEAGUE EAST CITIES

- NEW YORK
- PHILADELPHIA
- WASHINGTON, DC
- ATLANTA
- MIAMI

Area of Detail Shown

CANADA

UNITED STATES

MEXICO

When the Atlanta Braves played in the NL West division (1969–1993), three of their division rivals were located on the West Coast. Since the realignment in 1994, their division rivalries are now with East Coast teams only.

Braves were based on the East Coast, yet they played in the NL West division because they had previously been the Milwaukee Braves.

To form the new Central division, the Pittsburgh Pirates, St. Louis Cardinals, and Chicago Cubs were moved from the old NL East and grouped with the Cincinnati Reds and Houston Astros of the old NL West. The Braves were moved from the old NL West to the NL East, along with a new expansion team called the Florida Marlins. This made the NL East a five-team division, with the Braves, Marlins, New York

Mets, Philadelphia Phillies, and Montreal Expos. This lineup remained unchanged until 2005, when the Montreal Expos moved to Washington, D.C., and became the Washington Nationals.

As part of the 1994 realignment, Major League Baseball added an additional round of play-off games: the division play-offs. With the new arrangement, each National League division has a regular-season champion. These three teams move on the National League Division Series (NLDS). To round out the NLDS field, the division runner-up with the best record is awarded a play-off spot. This is the wild card team. Two best-of-five NLDS series are then played, with the winner of each series advancing to the National League Championship Series (NLCS).

Since the 1994 realignment, NL East teams have had tremendous success. NL East teams have won six NLCS, including the Atlanta Braves in 1995, 1996, and 1999; the New York Mets in 2000; and the Florida Marlins in 1997 and 2003. Three of those teams, the 1995 Braves and both Marlins teams, went on to win the World Series.

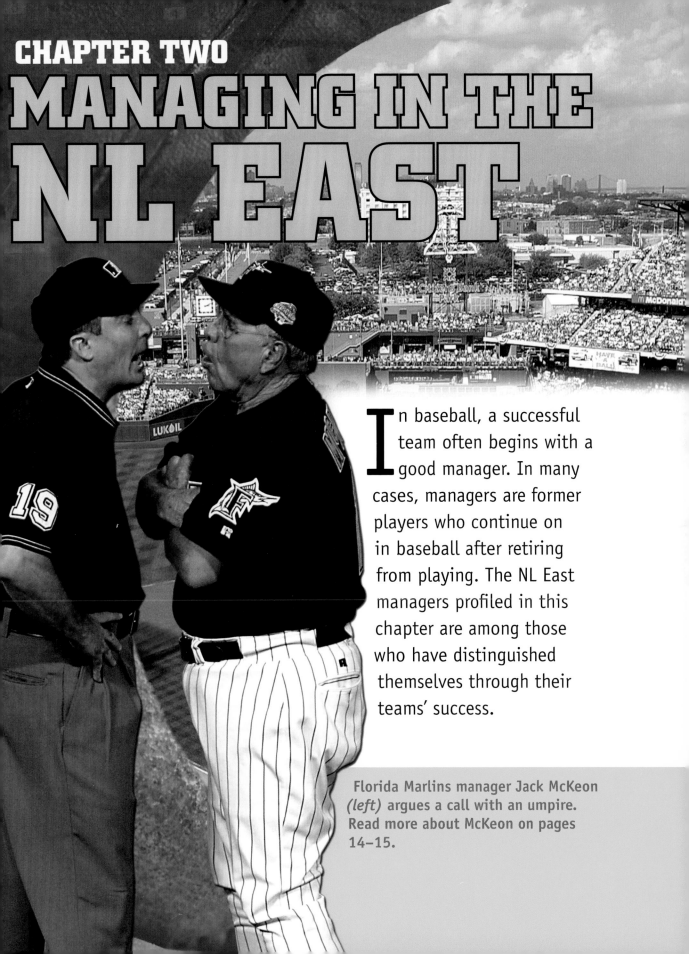

CHAPTER TWO
MANAGING IN THE NL EAST

In baseball, a successful team often begins with a good manager. In many cases, managers are former players who continue on in baseball after retiring from playing. The NL East managers profiled in this chapter are among those who have distinguished themselves through their teams' success.

Florida Marlins manager Jack McKeon *(left)* argues a call with an umpire. Read more about McKeon on pages 14–15.

Felipe Alou *(above)* coached his son Moises Alou in Montreal. Moises was an All-Star outfielder for five different National League teams, including the Expos.

Past NL East Managers

Felipe Alou managed the Montreal Expos from 1992 to 2001. Although the Expos never made it to the postseason under Alou, the manager earned high praise for getting the most out of his young, inexperienced teams. In 1994, Alou won the National League Manager of the Year Award, as his team had the best record in baseball when a players' strike ended the season prematurely.

Davey Johnson managed the New York Mets from 1981 to 1990. He guided them to a team record 108 victories and a World Series title in 1986. Johnson's Mets also made it to the NLCS in 1988, where they were beaten by the underdog Los Angeles Dodgers in seven games. He later managed the Cincinnati Reds and the Baltimore Orioles, winning the 1997 American League Manager of the Year Award with the Orioles.

Jack McKeon spent his career managing the Kansas City Royals, Oakland Athletics, San Diego Padres, and Cincinnati Reds before becoming manager of the Florida Marlins partway through the 2003 season. McKeon transformed the floundering team, leading it to the 2003 NL wild card and on to victory in the 2003 World Series against the New York Yankees. After the season, McKeon was named National League Manager of the Year for the second time, having previously won the award with Cincinnati in 1999. McKeon retired in 2005.

Frank Robinson and the Expos/Nationals

By the end of the 2001 season, the Montreal Expos franchise was on the brink of collapsing. After several losing seasons, they had one of the worst attendance records in baseball. The club needed a new owner, but no buyer was willing to invest in the team. Instead, Major League Baseball bought the team in order to keep it going until a decision about the franchise's future could be made.

For the 2002 season, Hall of Famer Frank Robinson was named manager of the Expos. Under difficult circumstances, he did what he could with the team. Robinson led the Expos to a winning record and a second-place finish in the NL East in 2002. He also led the team to a winning record in 2003. Major League Baseball then moved the Expos franchise to Washington, D.C., for the 2005 season, and Robinson continued to coach them through the transition. He left at the end of the 2006 season.

Robinson has one of the most complete resumes in all of baseball. While playing for the Cincinnati Reds, he won the 1956 Rookie of the Year Award, as well as the 1961 National League MVP Award. Five years later, he captured the 1966 American League MVP and World Series MVP while starring for the Baltimore Orioles. He has also been a player-manager, American League Manager of the Year (1989), Major League Baseball administrator, and team executive.

Other popular and successful coaches who led NL East teams include Jim Fregosi of the Philadelphia Phillies (1991–1996) and Bobby Valentine of the New York Mets (1996–2002).

Bobby Cox—Atlanta Braves

Bobby Cox is one of the most successful managers in baseball history. He first managed the Atlanta Braves from 1978 to 1981 but never

As of 2007, the Braves had won 14 NL East division titles under manager Bobby Cox. Here, he studies the field during the 2005 National League Division Series against the Houston Astros.

finished higher than fourth place. He then managed the Toronto Blue Jays for four seasons, helping them to a first-place finish in 1985 and winning his first Manager of the Year Award.

Cox returned to Atlanta as a manager in 1990, taking over a team that was only beginning to recover from years of mediocrity and failure. The Braves posted a losing record that season but miraculously finished in first place in the old NL West in 1991, going all the way to the World Series. Cox's Braves finished first in their division every season from 1991 to 2005, except for the strike-shortened 1994 season. During that streak, his teams advanced to the World Series five times—in 1991, 1992, 1995, 1996, and 1999. The Braves won the series in 1995 over the Cleveland Indians. As manager of the Braves, Cox has won the National League Manager of the Year Award three times, in 1991, 2004, and 2005. Through 2007, Cox had a 2,255–1,764 record.

Charlie Manuel—Philadelphia Phillies

Charlie Manuel managed the Cleveland Indians for three and a half seasons, from 2000 to 2002, leading them to a first-place finish in the AL Central in 2001. He took over the Philadelphia Phillies in 2005, taking the team to a second-place finish in the NL East with an 88–74 record. They finished second again in 2006 to the New York Mets. Although Manuel's Phillies began the 2007 season badly, the team managed to come back from a seven-game deficit behind the Mets to win the NL East in 2007 and make the play-offs for the first time since 1993. Through 2007, Manuel had a 482–417 managing record.

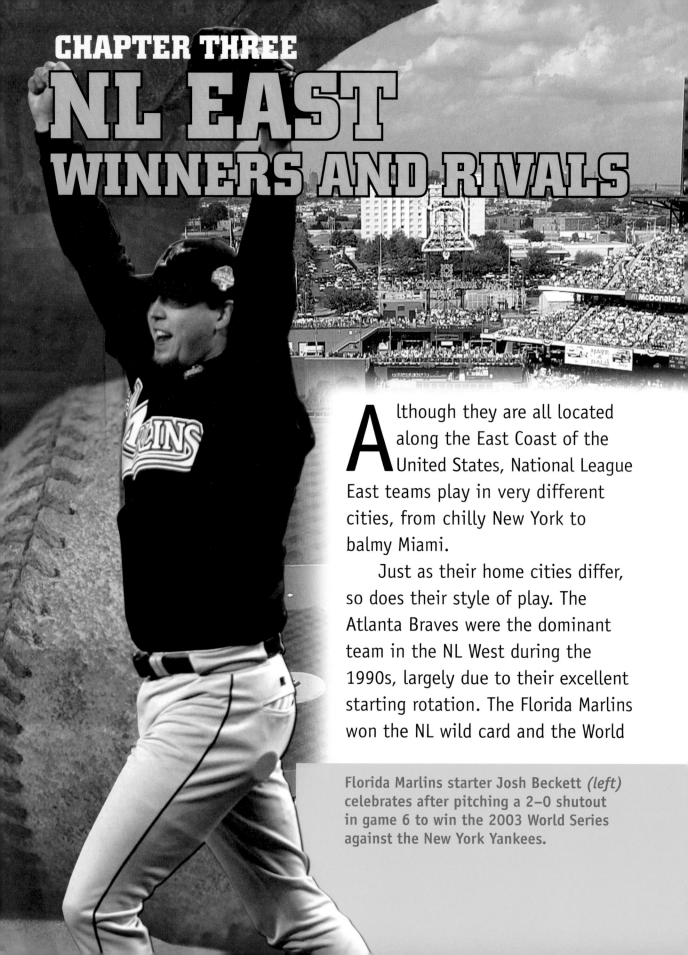

CHAPTER THREE
NL EAST
WINNERS AND RIVALS

Although they are all located along the East Coast of the United States, National League East teams play in very different cities, from chilly New York to balmy Miami.

Just as their home cities differ, so does their style of play. The Atlanta Braves were the dominant team in the NL West during the 1990s, largely due to their excellent starting rotation. The Florida Marlins won the NL wild card and the World

Florida Marlins starter Josh Beckett *(left)* celebrates after pitching a 2–0 shutout in game 6 to win the 2003 World Series against the New York Yankees.

Series in 1997 and 2003 with good pitching and a solid offense. Recently, the New York Mets and the Philadelphia Phillies have competed for the division championship with a combination of speed and slugging.

NL East Rivalries

Atlanta's recent dominance has fueled its rivalries with all the other teams in the division, but especially with the New York Mets. The Mets finished behind the Braves in the division every season through the 1990s. The home

Marlins shortstop Édgar Rentería completes a double play against the Cleveland Indians in game 7 of the 1997 World Series. Rentería later had the game-winning hit that clinched the series for Florida.

stretch of 1998 was particularly memorable, with the Mets failing to make the play-offs after losing a three-game series to the Braves near the end of the season. The Mets won the 1999 wild card and met the Braves in the NLCS, where the Braves beat them in six intense games. During the off-season that year, Braves closer John Rocker created a huge controversy by making derogatory comments about New York City in a *Sports Illustrated* interview. Extra security measures had to be taken when Rocker faced the Mets in New York during the 2000 season.

Atlanta Braves pitcher Steve Avery and New York Mets catcher Todd Hundley have to be separated by an umpire while they argue at home plate during a 1996 game. Avery had hit a Mets batter earlier in the game.

More recently, Philadelphia Phillies shortstop Jimmy Rollins helped develop a rivalry between his team and the Mets. Before the 2007 season began, Rollins declared the Phillies the team to beat in the NL East, despite the Mets winning the division in 2006. Rollins's prediction came true, as the Mets unraveled near the end of the season and were overtaken by the Phillies.

Other rivalries extend to interleague play. The New York Mets and the New York Yankees have a strong crosstown rivalry that was reenergized by the 2000 World Series, in which the Yankees beat the

Mets in five tense games. In one game, Yankees starting pitcher Roger Clemens threw part of a broken bat at Mets catcher Mike Piazza, nearly touching off a brawl.

The Nationals didn't arrive in Washington, D.C., until 2005, but they had already gained enemies within the Baltimore Orioles organization. For decades, the Orioles had been the only team in the D.C. area, and Orioles ownership tried hard to keep the Expos organization from moving to Washington. Though the two teams are in different leagues, they play two three-game series—called the Beltway Series—each year during interleague play.

The Team of the 1990s

From 1991 to 2005, the Atlanta Braves won their division 14 times, including 11 straight NL East titles. They appeared in the World Series five times during that stretch, winning it all in 1995. The Braves built their success around an excellent pitching staff that combined to win six Cy Young Awards, as well as a solid lineup that

Braves pitcher Tom Glavine gave up only one hit during his game 6 shutout against the Cleveland Indians in the 1995 World Series. It was his second win of the series.

included homegrown sluggers Chipper Jones and David Justice, Gold Glove outfielder Andruw Jones, and All-Star free-agent veterans such as first baseman Fred McGriff.

The 1995 team were relative underdogs going into the World Series, as they faced a Cleveland Indians team that won 100 games during the strike-shortened regular season. The Braves had lost back-to-back World Series in 1991 and 1992, and they lost the 1993 NLCS to Philadelphia. However, the Braves managed to outpitch the Indians in six close games, including a game 6 shutout by World Series MVP Tom Glavine. The Braves went on to two more World Series appearances in the decade, losing the 1996 series to the Yankees in six games and getting swept by the Yankees in 1999.

National League East Champs
(since 1994 realignment)

1994: Montreal Expos*
1995: Atlanta Braves
1996: Atlanta Braves
1997: Atlanta Braves
1998: Atlanta Braves
1999: Atlanta Braves
2000: Atlanta Braves
2001: Atlanta Braves
2002: Atlanta Braves
2003: Atlanta Braves
2004: Atlanta Braves
2005: Atlanta Braves
2006: New York Mets
2007: Philadelphia Phillies
* Strike-shortened season; no play-offs.

The Marlins and the Wild Card

In their first few seasons, the Florida Marlins finished with losing records. Then, for the 1997 season, the Marlins' owners made an effort to build a winning team. They added pitcher Alex Fernandez, outfielder Moises Alou, and third baseman Bobby Bonilla to a team that included young shortstop Édgar Rentería,

Dontrelle Willis of the Florida Marlins pitches against the New York Yankees in game 1 of the 2003 World Series. The rookie baffled Yankees batters with his great stuff and high leg kick.

All-Star outfielder Gary Sheffield, and ace starting pitcher Kevin Brown. Led by manager Jim Leyland, the Marlins finished the season nine games behind the Braves in the division, but their 92–70 record was good enough to earn them the National League wild card spot. The Marlins went on to beat the Braves 4–2 in the NLCS and advance to the World Series against Cleveland. "The Fish" won an exciting game 7 in extra innings to become the first wild card team to win the World Series.

The Marlins won their second wild card in 2003, behind strong starting pitching from Brad Penny, Josh Beckett, and Rookie of the Year

Dontrelle Willis. In addition, the team got solid hitting from veteran Gold Glove catcher Ivan Rodriguez, third baseman Miguel Cabrera, first baseman Derrek Lee, and outfielder Juan Pierre. In the National League Championship Series, the Marlins fell behind the Cubs three games to one before rallying to win the series in seven games. In the World Series, they beat the heavily favored New York Yankees in six games.

The Mets and the Phillies

Members of the Philadelphia Phillies celebrate after winning the NL East division in 2007. They beat the Washington Nationals on the last day of the season to clinch the title.

In 2006, the New York Mets finally broke Atlanta's streak of division championships, finishing 97–65, the best record in the National League. The Mets were well stocked with All-Stars, including outfielder Carlos Beltrán and young infielders José Reyes and David Wright. The Mets' pitching staff included former Cy Young Award winners Pedro Martinez and Tom Glavine, and closer Billy Wagner. The powerful Mets advanced to the NLCS, but they were beaten by the St. Louis Cardinals in seven games.

National League East Team History
(since realignment in 1994)

	YEAR ENTERED THE NL EAST	NL EAST CHAMPIONSHIPS	NATIONAL LEAGUE PENNANTS	WORLD SERIES CHAMPIONSHIPS
Atlanta Braves	1994	11	3	1
Florida Marlins	1994	0	2	2
New York Mets	1969	1	1	0
Philadelphia Phillies	1969	1	0	0
Washington Nationals*	1969	1**	0	0

* The Washington Nationals played as the Montreal Expos from 1969 to 2005.
** Includes 1994; Montreal was in first place in the division when the players' strike ended the season.

Continuing their regular-season success in 2007, the Mets led the division for much of the season. They had a seven-game lead over the Phillies with seventeen games left. But then, in perhaps the worst collapse in baseball history, the team lost 11 of their last 15 games. The Phillies, meanwhile, went 12–3 during the same stretch. They were led by MVP shortstop Jimmy Rollins, hot-hitting second baseman Chase Utley, All-Star outfielder Aaron Rowand, and slugging first baseman Ryan Howard. The Phillies clinched the division on the last day of the season, earning their first division title since 1993.

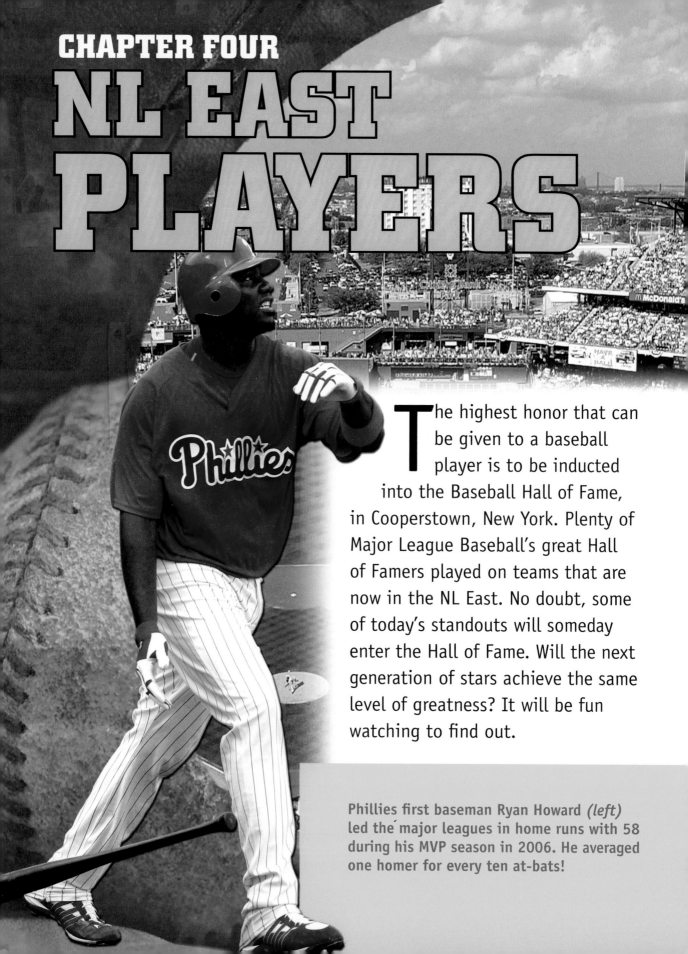

The highest honor that can be given to a baseball player is to be inducted into the Baseball Hall of Fame, in Cooperstown, New York. Plenty of Major League Baseball's great Hall of Famers played on teams that are now in the NL East. No doubt, some of today's standouts will someday enter the Hall of Fame. Will the next generation of stars achieve the same level of greatness? It will be fun watching to find out.

Phillies first baseman Ryan Howard *(left)* led the major leagues in home runs with 58 during his MVP season in 2006. He averaged one homer for every ten at-bats!

Past Greats from NL East Teams

Hank Aaron played for the Braves organization from 1954 to 1974, first in Milwaukee and then in Atlanta. He played on the Milwaukee Braves team that won the 1957 World Series and was named the 1957 National League MVP. An all-around great hitter, Aaron broke Babe Ruth's record of 714 career home runs in 1974. He retired with the Milwaukee Brewers in 1976 with 755 homers, a record that stood until Barry Bonds broke it in 2007. Aaron's record of 2,297 career RBI may never be broken, though. He was inducted into the Baseball Hall of Fame in 1982.

Tom Seaver of the New York Mets was the 1967 NL Rookie of the Year. He won the first of three Cy Young Awards in 1969, leading the underdog Mets to their first World Series championship. (See page 10.) He was traded to the Cincinnati Reds in 1977 and continued to pitch until retiring in 1987. Seaver started more opening-day games, 16, than any other pitcher in history. He finished his career with 311 wins, 3,640 strikeouts, and 61 shutouts. He was inducted into the Hall of Fame in 1992 with 98.8 percent of the ballots cast, the highest percentage ever.

Third baseman Mike Schmidt spent his entire career with the Philadelphia Phillies, from 1972 to 1989. Schmidt was a feared slugger who led the National League in home runs eight times. He was also an excellent fielder, winning ten Gold Glove Awards at third base. In 1980, Schmidt's Phillies defeated the Kansas City Royals to win their first World Series championship. The Phillies captain won his first National League MVP Award that year. He was also named MVP in 1981 and 1986. Schmidt retired in 1989 with 548 career home runs. He was inducted into the Hall of Fame in 1995.

NL East Stars, from 1994 to Present

In recent decades, players in the NL East have represented the division very well. Since the 1994 realignment, the division has produced three NL Most Valuable Player Award winners, while its pitchers have won the NL Cy Young Award seven times.

Atlanta Braves pitcher John Smoltz delivers a pitch during game 5 of the 1996 World Series against the New York Yankees.

Greg Maddux (Atlanta Braves), John Smoltz (Atlanta Braves), and Tom Glavine (Atlanta Braves, New York Mets)

From 1993 to 2002, the Atlanta Braves featured baseball's best starting rotation, including Greg Maddux, John Smoltz, and Tom Glavine. Together, the trio won five Cy Young Awards, nine division titles, three National League pennants, and a World Series.

Maddux joined the Braves in 1993, the season after winning his first Cy Young Award with the Chicago Cubs. As Atlanta's ace, he won three consecutive Cy Young Awards

(1993–1995). Maddux led the National League in ERA three times and in wins four times, including going 19–2 with a 1.63 ERA during the 1995 season. He left Atlanta in 2003 to join the Chicago Cubs, with whom he won his 300th game in 2004.

Smoltz enjoyed tremendous success as both a starting pitcher and as a closer for the Atlanta Braves. As a starter, he led the league in wins (24) and strikeouts (276) to win the 1996 Cy Young Award. The Braves converted him to a closer after he missed the 2000 season due to injuries. Smoltz responded well to the switch. In 2003, he led the league in saves (55) and earned the NL Rolaids Relief Man of the Year Award. He returned to Atlanta's starting rotation in 2005 and quickly reestablished himself as one of the best starters in the National League. Smoltz is the only pitcher in history to record 200 victories and 150 saves. He recorded his career strikeout number 3,000 in 2008.

Glavine pitched for the Braves from 1987 to 2002. He won 20 or more games for the Braves five times. Glavine won the NL Cy Young Award in 1991 and 1998, and was elected to ten All-Star teams. A successful postseason pitcher, Glavine was the MVP of the 1995 World Series against the Cleveland Indians. In the deciding sixth game, he pitched eight innings of one-hit ball to earn a 1–0 victory. He left the Braves and joined the Mets in 2003, helping New York reach the NLCS in 2006 and winning his 300th game in 2007. Glavine returned to the Braves after the 2007 season.

Pedro Martinez (Montreal Expos, New York Mets)

A hard-throwing strikeout pitcher, Pedro Martinez won the 1997 NL Cy Young Award while pitching for the Expos, going 17–8 with a 1.90 ERA and 305 strikeouts. He left the National League after that season to join the Boston Red Sox, with whom he won two more Cy Young

Awards and a World Series title. Martinez joined the New York Mets in 2005. He recorded the 3,000th strikeout of his career during the 2007 season, while pitching for the Mets.

Mike Piazza (New York Mets)

Mike Piazza began his major league career with the Los Angeles Dodgers and was named the National League's Rookie of the Year in 1993. In 1998, his first year with the Mets, Piazza hit .328, with 32 homers and 111 RBI. He went on to have several more excellent seasons with New York. Piazza made the NL All-Star team 12 times, including ten consecutive selections from 1993 to 2002. He left the Mets after the 2005 season to join the San Diego Padres.

Dontrelle Willis and Miguel Cabrera (Florida Marlins)

Dontrelle Willis and Miguel Cabrera began their careers together in 2003, playing for the eventual world champion Marlins. Willis went 14–6 to win the NL Rookie of the Year. Cabrera, for his part, made key hitting contributions to the team. After an off year, in 2005, Willis returned to form to lead the National League with 22 wins, while throwing five shutouts. The hard-hitting Cabrera represented the Marlins in the All-Star game four consecutive years (2004–2007). Unfortunately for Marlins fans, Willis and Cabrera were both traded to the Detroit Tigers of the American League after the 2007 season.

Jimmy Rollins (Philadelphia Phillies)

Jimmy Rollins debuted with the Phillies in 2000. Since then, he has established himself as one of the finest all-around shortstops in the major leagues. Already an All-Star, Rollins really broke out in the 2007 season. He became only the fourth player in major league history to

Slugger Mike Piazza hit 220 home runs while playing for the New York Mets. His 427 career homers are the most by a catcher in baseball history.

steal at least 20 bases and hit at least 20 home runs, doubles, and triples in a single season. Rollins finished with a career-high 30 home runs and 40 steals, while leading the Phillies to the 2007 play-offs. He won the 2007 National League MVP Award for his achievements and also earned his first Gold Glove Award for his slick fielding.

David Wright and José Reyes (New York Mets)

New York Mets fans have come to expect great things from their young infielders, third baseman David Wright and shortstop José Reyes. Wright finished the 2005, 2006, and 2007 seasons among the league

National League East Award Winners
(since realignment in 1994)

National League MVP Award
1999: Chipper Jones (Braves)
2006: Ryan Howard (Phillies)
2007: Jimmy Rollins (Phillies)

National League Rookie of the Year Award
2005: Ryan Howard (Phillies)
2006: Hanley Ramirez (Marlins)

National League Cy Young Award
1994: Greg Maddux (Braves)
1995: Greg Maddux (Braves)
1996: John Smoltz (Braves)
1997: Pedro Martinez (Expos)
1998: Tom Glavine (Braves)

Rolaids Relief Man of the Year Award
2000: Antonio Alfonseca (Marlins)
2001: Armando Benitez (Mets)
2002: John Smoltz (Braves)
2005: Chad Cordero (Nationals)

World Series MVP Award
1995: Tom Glavine (Braves)
1997: Livan Hernandez (Marlins)
2003: Josh Beckett (Marlins)

leaders in batting average and RBI. He made the All-Star team in 2006 and 2007, and also won his first Gold Glove Award in 2007.

José Reyes played his first full season for the Mets in 2005. He quickly established himself as a threat on the base paths, leading the National League in steals in 2005, 2006, and 2007, and regularly placing in the top ten in hits, runs, and at bats. He also led the NL in triples in 2005 and 2006, hitting 17 both seasons. Reyes was named to the 2006 and 2007 All-Star teams.

Mets shortstop José Reyes steals second in a 2007 game against the Milwaukee Brewers. His 78 steals that season were the most in the majors since the 1992 season.

Ryan Howard (Philadelphia Phillies)

After slugging 22 home runs in just 88 games, Phillies first baseman Ryan Howard was named National League Rookie of the Year in 2005. In 2006, he led the National League with 58 homers and 149 RBI to capture the NL MVP Award. He also made his first All-Star team and received the 2006 Hank Aaron Award, which is given to the league's best all-around hitter. Howard's average dropped in 2007, but he still managed to hit 47 homers and drive in 136 runs for the Phillies. The big-swinging slugger also struck out a record 199 times!

Hanley Ramirez (Florida Marlins)

In 2006, Marlins shortstop Hanley Ramirez announced his arrival on the scene by winning the National League Rookie of the Year Award. The following year, the Dominican-born star took his game to another level. His .332 batting average led the team, as did his 212 hits, 48 doubles, 359 total bases, and 125 runs scored. For good measure, Ramirez also slammed 29 home runs and swiped 51 bases. Early in the 2008 season, the Marlins and Ramirez agreed to the framework for a $70 million, six-year contract, so expect to see Ramirez in Marlins pinstripes for years to come.

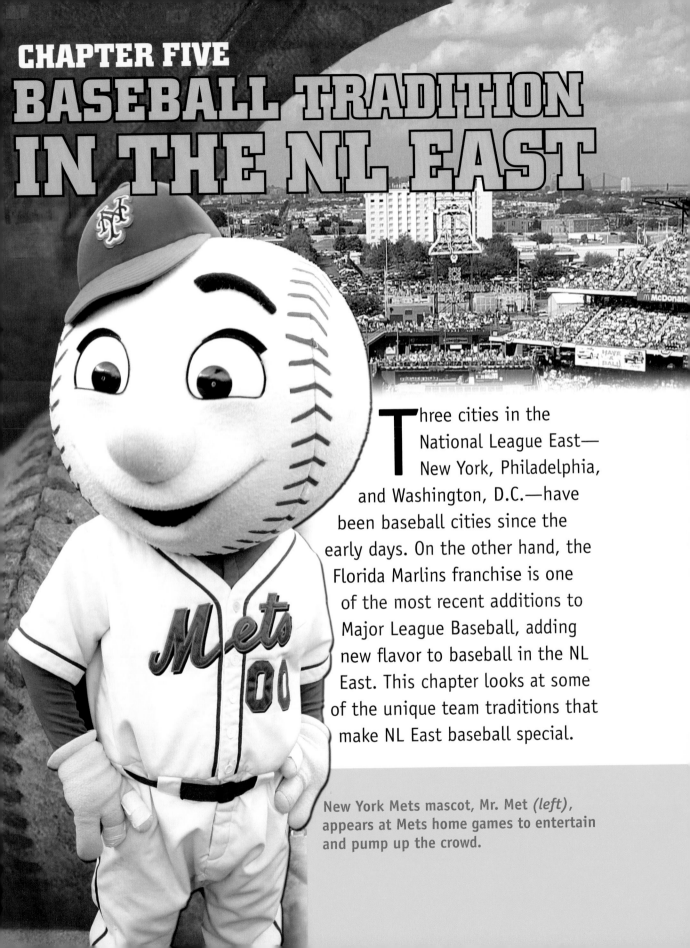

Three cities in the National League East—New York, Philadelphia, and Washington, D.C.—have been baseball cities since the early days. On the other hand, the Florida Marlins franchise is one of the most recent additions to Major League Baseball, adding new flavor to baseball in the NL East. This chapter looks at some of the unique team traditions that make NL East baseball special.

New York Mets mascot, Mr. Met (left), appears at Mets home games to entertain and pump up the crowd.

Atlanta Braves

The Braves are one of the oldest teams in Major League Baseball. The franchise was founded in 1871 as the Boston Red Stockings, becoming the Braves in 1912 but undergoing several more name changes until 1941. They played in Boston until 1953, when the team moved to Milwaukee, where they won the 1957 World Series. The team later moved to Atlanta, in 1966. The Braves are the only major league team to win a World Series title in three different cities, with the Boston Braves winning in 1914, the Milwaukee Braves winning in 1957, and the Atlanta Braves winning in 1995.

The Braves are sometimes called "America's Team." This nickname came about because of billionaire Ted Turner. The onetime Braves owner and cable television pioneer broadcast his team's games nation-wide on his cable network, TBS, before doing so became common. In 1976, less than one million people watched TBS. By 1982, more than 25 million households across the country had a full season of Braves games piped into their homes.

The Braves played in Atlanta's Fulton County Stadium from 1966 to 1996. The stadium was nicknamed "the Launching Pad" for the number of home runs hit in the park due to its shallow outfield. Today, the team plays at Turner Field, a stadium built just before Atlanta hosted the 1996 Olympic Games.

To get a rally going, fans in the stands sometimes do the "Tomahawk Chop," swinging their arms or plastic tomahawks while chanting. Some have criticized the Tomahawk Chop as being insulting to Native American culture. Supporters say it is just a fun way to get involved in the game.

Hall of Famer Gary Carter

Catcher Gary Carter was an 11-time All-Star who spent most of his career with the Montreal Expos and the New York Mets. He was inducted into the Baseball Hall of Fame in 2003. Usually, players who have been with more than one team can decide which team they want to represent on their plaque. Carter began his career in Montreal and spent 12 seasons with the Expos. Though he played on the Mets for only five seasons, he helped the team win the 1986 World Series. Carter decided that he wanted to be shown wearing a New York cap, or a cap with a split logo representing Montreal on one side and New York on the other. Officials at the Hall of Fame, however, didn't have any players representing Montreal. In the end, they went against Carter's wishes and showed him in an Expos cap. Carter remains Montreal's lone representative in the Baseball Hall of Fame.

Gary Carter spent 12 of his 19 seasons in the majors north of the border, playing for the Montreal Expos.

Florida Marlins

The Marlins are the newest franchise in the NL East, having entered as an expansion team in 1993. Fans often refer to the Marlins as "the Fish." Though the Marlins have won two World Series titles, they have never finished first in their division.

For the first 18 seasons, the Marlins played in cavernous Dolphins Stadium, which was built mostly to accommodate football. Despite postseason success, the team has sometimes failed to attract fans. For a brief period, there was talk of moving the team or even closing the franchise. This talk came to an end when the Marlins announced their plans to build a new Marlins Stadium in time for the 2011 season.

New York Mets

Citi Field, the new ballpark for the New York Mets, is shown under construction beside Shea Stadium in a 2007 aerial photo.

The Mets were founded in New York City in 1962 as an expansion team, filling a gap created when the Brooklyn Dodgers moved to Los Angeles and the New York Giants moved to San Francisco in the 1950s. Once again, New York City had a baseball team in each league and a crosstown rivalry (Mets–Yankees). The Mets played in Shea Stadium—located in the New York borough of Queens—from 1964 to 2008. Their new park, Citi Field, was built alongside Shea Stadium.

The Mets name comes from a shortening of the word "Metropolitan," the name for a New York baseball team from the 1880s. Their mascot is Mr. Met, a costumed character with a baseball for a head. Their inter-locking "NY" logo is taken from the old logo of the New York Giants baseball team. The team's full logo shows a New York skyline featuring several prominent city landmarks, including the Empire State Building and the Williamsburg Bridge.

Philadelphia Phillies

The Phillies name comes from a shortening of the team's early nickname, the "Philadelphians." For years, the Phillies played at Veterans Stadium. In 2004, "the Vet," as it was known, was demolished and the Phillies moved into the new Citizens Bank Park. Despite being one of baseball's old-est franchises, the Phillies have won only one World Series title, in 1980. (In 2007, the Phillies became the first professional sports franchise in North America to lose 10,000 games!)

The Philadelphia Phillies opened their beautiful new Citizens Bank Park in 2004 with an 8–4 victory over the Washington Nationals.

Philadelphia has one of the most unforgiving fan bases in sports. Fans threw batteries at Los Angeles Dodgers pitcher Burt Hooton during the 1977 National League Championship Series, and Phillies reliever Mitch Williams received death threats after losing the final game of the 1993 World Series to the Toronto Blue Jays. In recent years, some fans have tried to soften this image. In a notable tradition carried over from the old Veterans Stadium, die-hard Phillies fan groups at Citizens Bank Park sit together to cheer for their "Phan Phavorites." For example, Jimmy Rollins's fans call themselves "J-Rolls Bakery," while fans of Chase Utley are called "Utley's Uglies."

Washington Nationals

The Washington Nationals franchise was originally the Montreal Expos. That team was formed in Canada as part of Major League Baseball's 1969 expansion. After decades of failing to attract fans or field winning teams, the Expos moved to Washington, D.C., in 2005. In 2003 and 2004, the franchise's final years as the Montreal Expos, the team actually played some home games in San Juan, Puerto Rico. As hoped, these games attracted far more fans than most Montreal home games.

The Nationals are the first major league team to play in Washington since the Senators franchise left in 1972 to become the Texas Rangers. The Nationals' nickname comes from two former Washington teams, who used it interchangeably with the Senators. Fans often call them the Nats. For their first three seasons, the Nationals played in RFK Stadium, home of the Washington Redskins football team. The Nats' new home—Nationals Stadium—opened on the first day of the 2008 season with President George W. Bush throwing out the first pitch. The team has never played in the World Series, either as the Expos or as the Nationals.

GLOSSARY

closer Relief pitcher who can protect a close lead for an inning or two at the end of a baseball game.

derogatory Expressing a low opinion; insulting.

earned run average (ERA) Statistic indicating the average number of earned runs scored per game against a pitcher.

formidable Strong, fearsome.

franchise In baseball, an organization or team, along with its name and logo.

Gold Glove In major league baseball, an award given every year to the best defender at each position.

inept Clumsy and prone to failure.

lineup A list of batters in the order in which they will bat.

mediocrity Averageness; the quality of not being outstanding.

plaque Flat, thin piece of metal with an inscription and/or engraving used for commemorative purposes.

quirk Irregularity or oddity.

rookie Someone who is new to a job or situation.

save Baseball statistic, awarded to the relief pitcher who preserves a close lead at the end of a game.

scout In baseball, a person whose job it is to assess the abilities of players.

shutout In baseball, a game in which one team fails to score.

tumultuous Wild and stormy.

Major League Baseball
The Office of the Commissioner of Baseball
245 Park Avenue, 31st Floor
New York, NY 10167
(212) 931-7800
Web site: http://www.mlb.com
The commissioner's office oversees all aspects of Major League
    Baseball.

National Baseball Hall of Fame and Museum
25 Main Street
Cooperstown, NY 13326
(888) HALL-OF-FAME (425-5633)
Web site: http://www.baseballhalloffame.org
The National Baseball Hall of Fame and Museum celebrates
    and preserves the history of baseball.

Negro Leagues Baseball Museum
1616 East 18th Street
Kansas City, MO 64108
(816) 221-1920
Web site: http://www.nlbm.com
The Negro Leagues Baseball Museum honors great African
    American baseball players who were once excluded from
    Major League Baseball.

(Note: Links to official individual team Web sites are available at the Rosenlinks URL, listed below.)

Web Sites

Due to the changing nature of Internet links, Rosen Publishing has developed an online list of Web sites related to the subject of this book. This site is updated regularly. Please use this link to access the list:

http://www.rosenlinks.com/imlb/nale

Adell, Ross, and Ken Samelson. *Amazing Mets Trivia*. Lanham, MD: Taylor Trade Publishing, 2004.

Altergott, Hannah. *Great Teams in Baseball History*. Milwaukee, WI: Raintree Publishing, 2006.

Forker, Dom, et al. *Baffling Baseball Trivia*. Madison, WI: Main Street Press, 2004.

Formosa, Dan, and Paul Hamburger. *Baseball Field Guide: An In-Depth Illustrated Guide to the Complete Rules of Baseball*. New York, NY: Thunder's Mouth Press, 2006.

Frommer, Frederic J. *The Washington Nationals 1859 to Today: The Story of Baseball in the Nation's Capital*. Lanham, MD: Taylor Trade Publishing, 2006.

Green, Ron, Jr. *101 Reasons to Love the Braves*. New York, NY: Stewart, Tabori & Chang, 2008.

Green, Ron, Jr., and David M. Jordan. *Occasional Glory: The History of the Philadelphia Phillies*. Jefferson, NC: McFarland & Company, Inc., 2003.

Light, Jonathan Fraser. *The Cultural Encyclopedia of Baseball*. Jefferson, NC: McFarland & Company, Inc., 2005.

Thorn, John, ed., et al. *Total Baseball, Completely Revised and Updated: The Ultimate Baseball Encyclopedia*. Wilmington, DE: SportClassic Books, 2004.

Westcott, Rich. *Phillies Essential: Everything You Need to Know to Be a Real Fan!* Chicago, IL: Triumph Books, 2006.

BIBLIOGRAPHY

Alvarez, Mark, ed. *The Perfect Game*. Dallas, TX: The Taylor
Publishing Company, 2003.

Blum, Ronald. "Baseball Owners Give Conditional Approval
to Expos' Move to Washington." *USA Today*, December 3,
2004. Retrieved April 15, 2008 (http://www.usatoday.
com/sports/baseball/nl/expos/2004-12-03-washington-
move_x.htm).

Bryson, Michael G. *The Twenty-Four-Inch Home Run and Other
Outlandish, Incredible but True Events in Baseball History*.
Chicago, IL: Contemporary Books, 1990.

ESPN.com. "Owners Approve 22-Game Slate in Puerto Rico."
November 20, 2008. Retrieved April 15, 2008 (http://
espn.go.com/mlb/news/2002/1120/1463782.html).

Foreman, Sean. "Major League Baseball Statistics and History."
Baseball-Reference.com. Retrieved April 15, 2008 (http://
www.baseball-reference.com).

Frisaro, Joe. "Second to None: Marlins Win It All!" MLB.com,
October 25, 2003. Retrieved April 15, 2008 (http://mlb.
mlb.com/mlb/ps/y2003/index.jsp).

Goldman, Steve, ed. *It Ain't Over 'Til It's Over: The Baseball
Prospectus Pennant Race Book*. New York, NY: Perseus
Book Group, 2007.

Koppett, Leonard. *Koppett's Concise History of Major League
Baseball*. New York, NY: Carroll & Graf Publishers, 2004.

Kuenster, John. *Heartbreakers: Baseball's Most Agonizing Defeats*. Chicago, IL: Ivan R. Dee Publisher, 2001.

MLB.com. "Dolphins Stadium." 2008. Retrieved May 9, 2008 (http://florida.marlins.mlb.com/fla/ballpark/index.jsp).

MLB.com. "History of the Game: From Doubleday to Present Day." 2008. Retrieved April 15, 2008 (http://mlb.mlb.com/mlb/history/index.jsp).

MLB.com. "Nationals Park." 2008. Retrieved May 9, 2008 (http://nationals.mlb.com/was/ballpark/index.jsp).

MLB.com. "Not Your Typical Ballpark." 2008. Retrieved May 9, 2008 (http://phillies.mlb.com/phi/ballpark/not_your_typical_ballpark.jsp).

MLB.com. "Welcome to Turner Field." 2008. Retrieved May 9, 2008 (http://atlanta.braves.mlb.com/atl/ballpark/index.jsp).

O'Connell, Kevin, and Josh Pahigian. *The Ultimate Baseball Road-Trip: A Fan's Guide to Major League Stadiums*. Guilford, CT: The Lyons Press, 2004.

Sheinin, Dave. "Collapse Is Complete, and the Mets Are History." *Washington Post*, October 1, 2007. Retrieved April 15, 2008 (http://www.washingtonpost.com/wp-dyn/content/article/2007/09/30/AR2007093000262.html).

Stevenson, Jim. "Baseball Opening Day: DC Team Inaugurates New Stadium with Win." *Voice of America News*, March 31, 2008. Retrieved April 15, 2008 (http://www.voanews.com/english/2008-03-31-voa12.cfm).

Zolecki, Todd. "Phillies' Rollins Named NL MVP." *Philadelphia Inquirer*, November 20, 2007. Retrieved April 15, 2008 (http://www.philly.com/philly/hp/sports/20071120_Phillies_Rollins_named_NL_MVP.html).

INDEX

A

Aaron, Hank, 10, 27, 34
Alou, Felipe, 14
Atlanta Braves, 4, 5, 9–11, 12, 16–17,
    18, 19, 21–22, 23, 24, 28–29, 36

B

Baseball Hall of Fame, 26, 27, 37
Beckett, Josh, 4, 23

C

Cabrera, Miguel, 24, 30
Carter, Gary, 37
Cox, Bobby, 16–17

F

Florida Marlins, 4, 5, 11, 12, 15, 18,
    22–24, 30, 34, 35, 37–38

G

Glavine, Tom, 22, 24, 28

H

Howard, Ryan, 25, 34

J

Johnson, Davey, 14

M

Maddux, Greg, 28–29

Manuel, Charlie, 17
Martinez, Pedro, 24, 29–30
McKeon, Jack, 14–15
Montreal Expos, 9, 12, 14, 15, 21, 29,
    37, 40

N

National League
    history of, 7–12
    1994 realignment, 9–12
National League Championship Series, 9,
    10, 14, 19, 22, 23, 24, 29, 40
National League East division
    managers of, 13–17
    players of, 26–34
    rivalries of, 19–21
    traditions in, 35–40
New York Mets, 4, 6, 9, 10, 11–12, 14,
    16, 17, 19, 20–21, 24–25, 27, 29,
    30, 32–33, 35, 37, 38–39

P

Philadelphia Phillies, 4, 5, 6, 7, 9, 11,
    16, 17, 19, 20, 22, 25, 27, 30–32,
    34, 35, 39–40
Piazza, Mike, 21, 30

R

Ramirez, Hanley, 34
Reyes, José, 24, 32, 33
Robinson, Frank, 15
Rollins, Jimmy, 20, 25, 30–32, 40

S

Schmidt, Mike, 27
Seaver, Tom, 10, 27
Smoltz, John, 28, 29

U

Utley, Chase, 25, 40

W

Washington Nationals, 4, 5, 12, 15, 21, 35, 40
Willis, Dontrelle, 24, 30
World Series, 4–5, 8, 9, 10, 14, 15, 17, 19, 20, 21, 22, 23, 24, 27, 28, 29, 30, 36, 37, 39, 40
Wright, David, 24, 32–33

About the Author

Jason Porterfield is a writer living in Chicago. He has authored more than 20 books for Rosen Publishing, covering topics from American history to college basketball. His sports titles for Rosen include *Baseball: Rules, Tips, Strategy, and Safety*; *Kurt Busch: NASCAR Driver*; *Basketball in the ACC (Atlantic Coast Conference)*; and *Basketball in the Big East Conference*.

Photo Credits

Designer: Sam Zavieh; Editor: Christopher Roberts; Photo Researcher: Cindy Reiman